THIS WALKER BOOK BELONGS TO:

_____

_____

_____

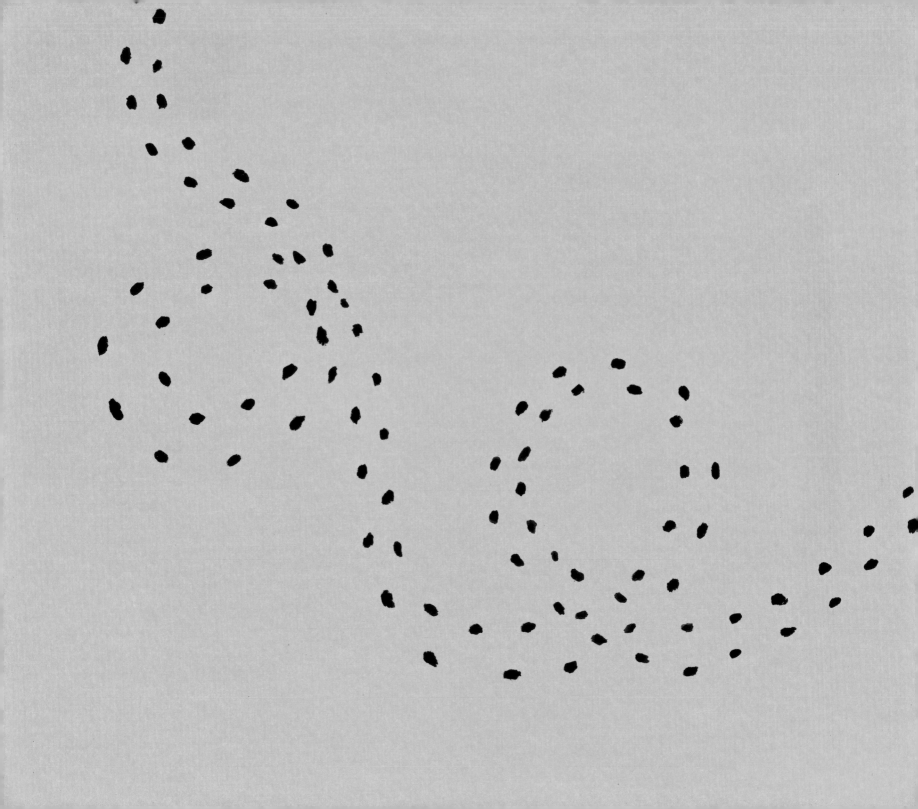

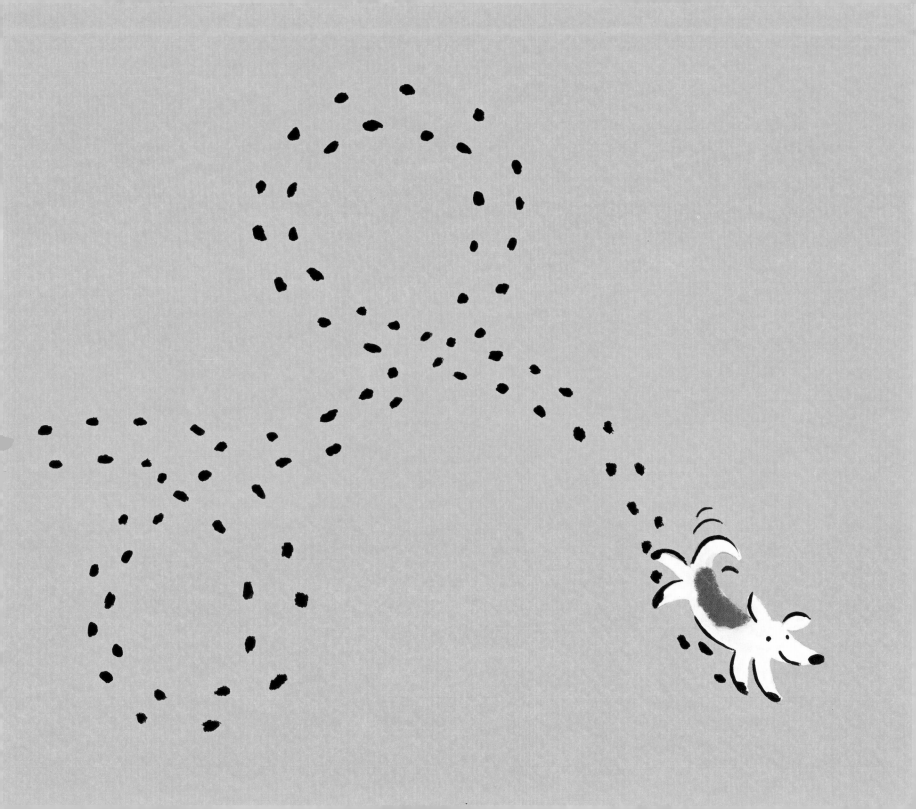

For Georgia
and Theo

First published 2003 by Walker Books Ltd
87 Vauxhall Walk, London SE11 5HJ

This edition published 2004

2 4 6 8 10 9 7 5 3 1

© 2003 Sarah McMenemy

The right of Sarah McMenemy to be identified as author/illustrator of this work has been asserted by her in accordance with the Copyright, Designs and Patents Act 1988

This book has been typeset in AT Arta Medium

Printed in China

British Library Cataloguing in Publication Data: a catalogue record for this book is available from the British Library   ISBN 1-84428-480-8

www.walkerbooks.co.uk

WALKER BOOKS
AND SUBSIDIARIES
LONDON · BOSTON · SYDNEY · AUCKLAND

Waggle

Sarah McMenemy

One day
Rosie's dad
came home
early.

"Look what I've
got," he said.

"A puppy!"
cried Rosie.

The puppy was small and furry,
with a black nose,
a brown patch and a very
waggly tail ...

and he wanted
to play.

The puppy thought everything was exciting,

especially the shoes.

He gave one to Rosie. "I've never played
Flip-flop before," said Rosie.
"Flip-flop, Flip-flop."

"Woof,
woof,
woof,"
barked
the puppy.

Then
the puppy found
a wastepaper
basket.

"Can I
play too?"
asked Rosie.

"Woof,"

barked the puppy.
He thought Rosie
looked funny
and he waggled his tail.

"Come on, puppy, let's go
into the garden," said Rosie.

"I think you'll like gardening. I'm sure you are
a good digger. Digger, dig, dig!" she shouted.
Waggle, waggle, waggle, went the puppy's tail.

"Let's go really fast," called Rosie.

Crash! Splash!

"This is a very muddy puddle,"
laughed Rosie.

"Woof, woof, **woof**,"
agreed the puppy.

Dad was calling, so they ran indoors.

"What a mess," he laughed. "I can see you've been having fun."

"Yes," said Rosie. "I love the puppy."

"What do you think
we should call him?"
asked Dad.

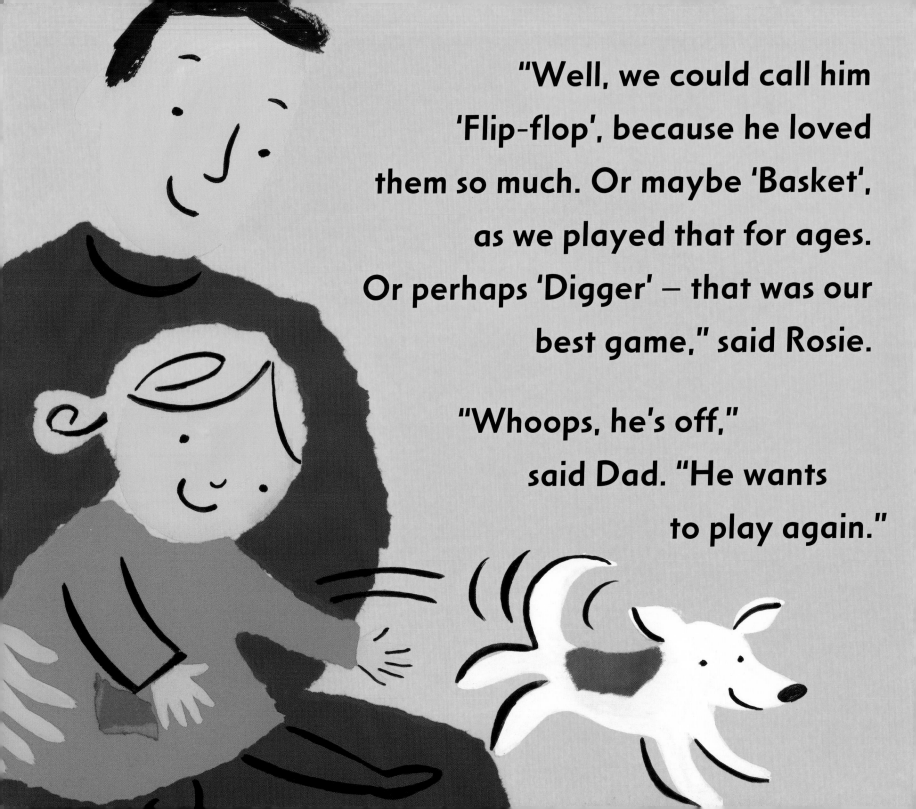

"Well, we could call him 'Flip-flop', because he loved them so much. Or maybe 'Basket', as we played that for ages. Or perhaps 'Digger' – that was our best game," said Rosie.

"Whoops, he's off," said Dad. "He wants to play again."

They followed
  the puppy
as he ran up
  the stairs ...

 and into Mum
and Dad's bedroom.

leapt onto the bed ...

and out
again ...

He jumped over the chair ...

ran under the table ...

scurried into the wardrobe ...

and raced out of the room.

Rosie raced after him.

"Where are you, puppy?" she called.

"Puppy! Puppy!" she shouted.

She looked everywhere.

"Puppy, come out!"
she said. Then she looked
towards the window.
The curtain was waggling.

Waggle, waggle, **waggle!**

Rosie pulled back the curtain and the puppy jumped into her arms. "I saw your tail waggling," said Rosie. "That's how I found you."

"Look, his tail is still waggling," said Dad.
"It hasn't stopped since he arrived."
Rosie looked at the puppy. "I think we
should call you 'Waggle'," she said.
"Do you like that name?"

And Waggle

    licked her nose

as if to say ...

yes.

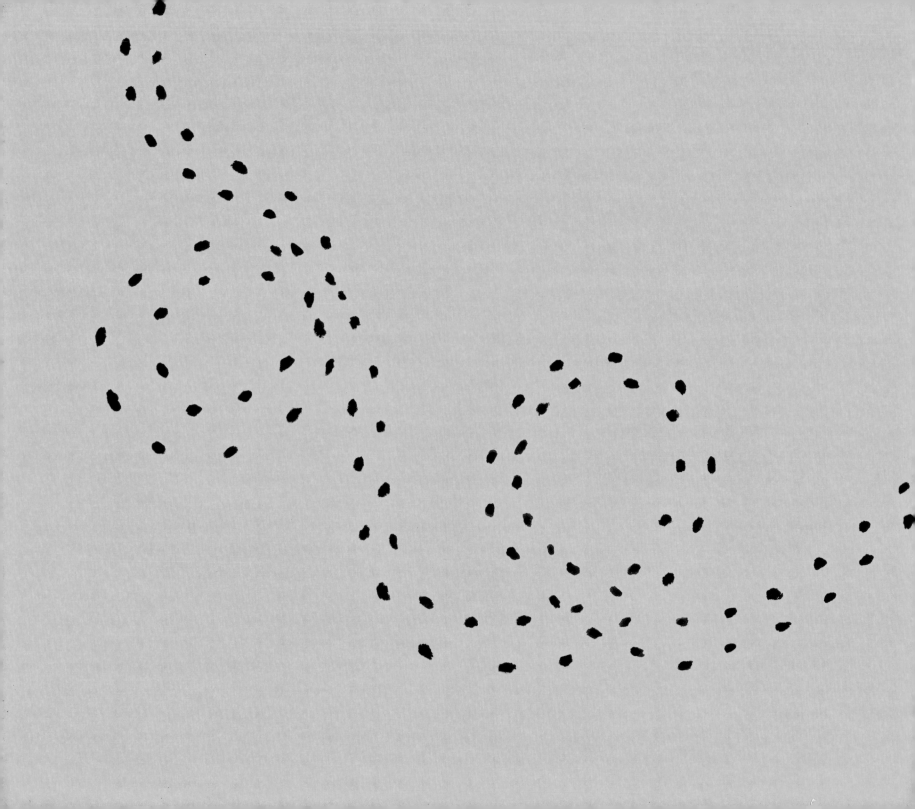

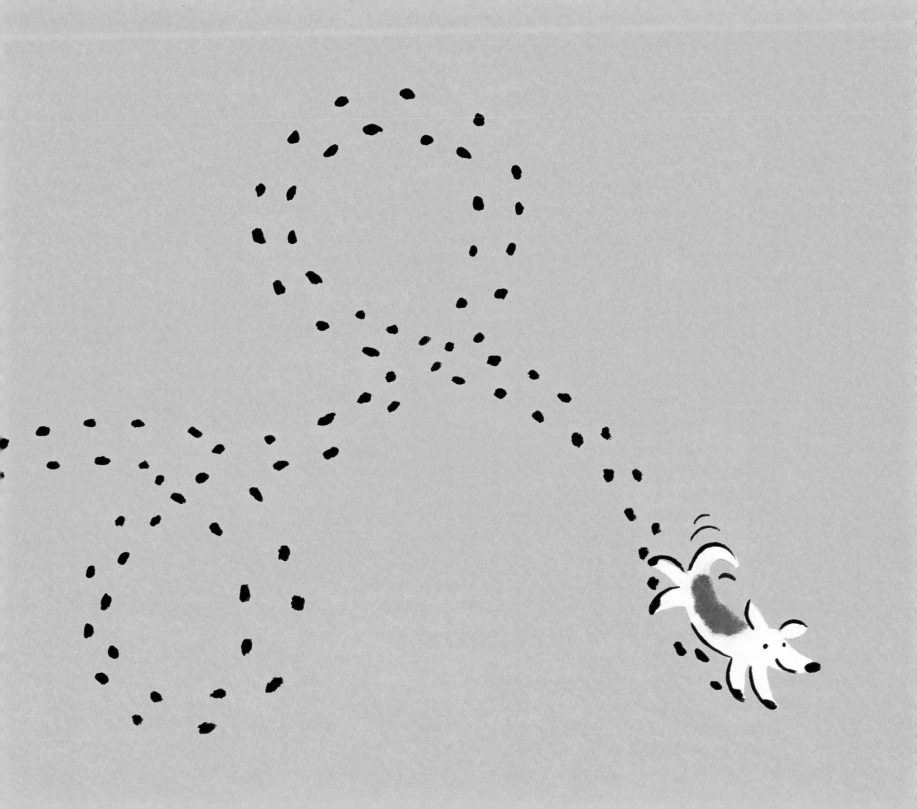

WALKER BOOKS is the world's leading independent
publisher of children's books. Working with
the best authors and illustrators we create books
for all ages, from babies to teenagers – books your child
will grow up with and always remember. So…

FOR THE BEST CHILDREN'S BOOKS, LOOK FOR THE BEAR